Henry L. Turner, W. De Meza, Myra Manley

Into Death's Country

Henry L. Turner, W. De Meza, Myra Manley

Into Death's Country

ISBN/EAN: 9783337300449

Printed in Europe, USA, Canada, Australia, Japan

Cover: Foto ©Andreas Hilbeck / pixelio.de

More available books at **www.hansebooks.com**

INTO DEATH'S COUNTRY.

Henry Lathrop Turner

ILLUSTRATED BY
MYRA MANLEY AND W DE MEZA

KNIGHT & LEONARD, PRINTERS,
CHICAGO.

CONTENTS:

THE LEGENDS TELL US OF A WONDROUS TREE WHICH
BORE A LEAF OF RICH AND RARE PERFUME, AND EVER
WHEN IT GAVE A LEAF TWO OTHERS SPRANG FULL
GROWN INTO THE VACANT PLACE. BUT LIFE THE LEG-
END FAR OUTDOES, FOR WHEN WE GIVE A JOY A
THOUSAND JOYS MAKE GOOD THE LOSS. IF IT MIGHT
HAPPEN THAT THIS LITTLE GIFT SHOULD BEAR SOME
HAPPINESS OR COMFORT IN ITS TRAIN, THEN WOULD A
MULTITUDE OF SWIFT-WINGED PLEASURES SPEED THEIR
HOMEWARD WAY.

THE CLOSING DAY.

THE CLOSING DAY.

BEYOND the mesa's rolling crest
  A golden day is closing,
And far within the crimson west
One snowy cloud 's reposing.

A single gem of night's fair crown
Shines dimly o'er the mountain,
As twilight settles softly down
O'er forest, field and fountain.

A sad wind breathes from far away
And 'mongst the palms is grieving,
While o'er the hills the dying day
A violet glory 's weaving.

THE CLOSING DAY.

The restless sea its surging tide
Hurls on with angry roaring.
With whistling cry and wings thrown wide
A white gull 's swiftly soaring.

Within a cottage waning low
A golden life is closing,
And soul as white as cloud of snow
On Faith's warm breast 's reposing.

And never shone in starry night,
Of myriad gems in cluster,
So clear, so pure, so calm a light
As that soul's dying luster.

Day softly beckons unto Night,
Life unto Death seems calling,
While o'er Time's every mountain height
A gracious memory's falling.

The Passing of a Soul

THE PASSING OF A SOUL.

SWEET friends, whom I love so tenderly, fondly,
  Yon glorious sun that swiftly is setting
Will never, ah! nevermore rise for me.
Life draws to its close, and soon I must leave you
And pass from your sight to Death's country.
My lingering soul, as it bids you adieu,
Would rest in your love through the pathos of parting,
And down through the crystalline depths of your eyes

THE PASSING OF A SOUL.

Would mark the fair lines of the undying spirit;
By its love, or its strength, or its beauty,
By its shyness, its grace, or its sweetness,
Engraft in my thought each charm and endearment
That shall blossom hereafter unfading, immortal,
That happily thus I may never forget you,
But when you shall follow me on to Death's country,
I may know you and welcome you warmly.

Ah! know you, dear friends, how fondly I hold you
Enshrined in my heart with the others, the absent,
Who over my life in this land of the sunset
Have wrought a fair day without storm cloud or shadow?

My soul is in sorrow with tender regretting
At parting from friends and my dearly loved home.
O, luminous land! O, beautiful country!
How fair grow its charms to eyes that are closing!
With its softness of summer unbroken, unending,
With the sheen of its stars and its unfailing sunlight,
With the blue of its sky and its ocean;
Buttressed with mountains so bold and so rugged,
That circle from seaward far on towards the sunrise;
Cut deeply and sharply by burrowing cañons,
My cool, shady, evergreen cañons,
Which restfully soothe in their stillness and shadows
Life's hurrying fever and endless endeavor;
With its orange groves, palm trees and poppies,
My sun-embossed, golden-lipped poppies;
Farewell to thee, dear sunny home,
It is farewell and farewell forever.

THE PASSING OF A SOUL.

What step heard I then just under the palm tree?
Was it thine, O, my peerless, my priceless, my beauty?

Shall I never, ah! nevermore spring to the saddle,
Or thrill to thy free spirit bounding beneath me?
Is it good-bye and good-bye forever?

Just see how he longingly looks for his mistress,
And oh! he is calling me—calling,
As many a time he will call without answer.

How well I remember the day
When, chased by the tide's rapid flowing,
We flew down the beach from the point
Where the big beetling crag of asphaltum
Glooms down like the black shade of Erebus.
'Twas when the wild beauty was still unconverted,
Ere yet he had come to be fond of his mistress,
Or had learned to be gentle and gracious.
Like a will-o-the-wisp in the twilight,
Like a firefly under the saddle,
He swerved at the roar of the breakers,
Or wheeled with the swiftness of light
At the uplifting flight of the heron.

The sun, dipping low down the turbulent sky,
Emblazoned the sea with a fierce, tossing glory
Of pink and of gray and of deep tinted purple.

Santa Cruz towered up phantom-like and uncanny,
Half mists and half mountain and island;
The cliffs at the left growing weird in the twilight,
Seemed cruelly crowding us into the ocean.
Still narrower ever our pathway was growing,
The white tongues of spray thrusting spitefully upward
And borne on the breeze the salt breath of the breaker
As we rode a mad race through the gathering shadows
'Gainst the encroaching tide and night's coming.

O, my peerless, my starry-eyed beauty!
Is it never to feel—ah, the sorrow!
Thy gentle neck rest on my shoulder?
Is it good-bye for aye and forever?
Or wilt thou yet follow and find me
Away in the realms of Death's country,
And bear me with joy o'er the hills—
The evergreen hills
Of the golden Hereafter,
Or sweep down the echoing shores
Of the Eternal Ocean?

THE PASSING OF A SOUL.

Draw me the curtains aside,
And set wide the half-open door;
Once more would I look to the hills
Whence cometh my courage and help.

O, my glorious, many-hued mountains!
Green, where the mist and the dew
Have found little patches of verdure,
And brown where the brawn of the rock
Lieth bare to the winds and the weather.
And see, how the far setting sun
Is touching them deftly and softly
With a haze of the rich, mellow amber,
Whilst the frowning and crestfallen shadows
Steal away to the sheltering cañons.

And mark you, how stealthily now
Through the amber of daylight
The night tints are creeping,
The grays and the violets
The bright gold o'erlapping.

O! ye great solemn heights!
How often in times of depression,
Of doubt or of bitterest sorrow,
Have I found in thy protecting presence
Courage and calmness and solace.

How well I remember the radiant day
We climbed through the chapparal's maze to the peak

Of the point hitherward from San Marcus.
The tortuous trail had grown fainter and blinder,
The bald, broken rocks grew more rugged and bolder,
As we rode through the glorious, life-giving sunlight,
Engrossed in light converse and free-hearted laughter,
Or deep in the problem of life and the future;
'Till the climbing grew stiffer and wilder and steeper,
'Till my laboring mount and the big Tam O'Shanter,
As they worked their way toilsomely upward,
Seemed to cling to the breast of the uncovered rock,
As a fly to the face of a window.
And though all my heart was in doubting and tremor,
I would not be frightened or daunted.
But, oh! when at length we had gained the far summit
A scene out of fairy-land burst on our vision!
Beneath us the rocks of the bluff Santa Yñes,
Whilst through the blue haze that fell o'er their summits
Away to the North swept the brown San Rafael.
Rivals they stood in the great things of nature,
They, the twin ranges of mountains;
While down, down between like a wandering starbeam,
Now bright, clear and glittering, now dull, gray and darkling,
As first the sun touched it, then shadow,
Ran a stream to the welcoming ocean.
And southward far off in the distance below us
Lay in sunlight the silent, the virginal valley,
And beyond it the sea with an unruffled surface,
And out in the sea the weird Santa Rosa,
Embosomed in vapors dim, mystic and ghostly,
Whilst on, ever on, stretched the glistening sea

Until where the dazzled and wearying eye
Swept away to its uttermost limit,
The silvery mists like a translucent veil
Fell glistening down from the heavens.

O, tenderest hearts, how sweetly, how kindly,
You've followed and cheered me adown the dark valley!
But now I must part from you, lingeringly, sadly,
For through the hot tears the darkness is pressing
And robbing my sight of your dear, loving presence.
I would that my vision could pierce the dim future
And follow through all of the infinite distance
The narrowing lines of its fading perspective.
But I know we shall meet in the happy Hereafter,
And in the fair aisles of some beautiful Aiden,
Through a lengthening vista of shining to-morrows,
In joy we'll forget the sad sorrow of parting,
And know but the blissful delight of reunion.

As on the sea some lonely ship,
With white sails swelling in the wind
And tall masts bending to their will,
Passes within the silvery mists,
Which sun nor moon nor sight can pierce,
All trusting to the helmsman's skill —
So I, O! great Omnipotent!
Thus resting on Thy love and power,
Launch out into the vast Unknown
And yield my soul unto Thy hand.

Ah, "when to dying eyes
The casement slowly grows

THE PASSING OF A SOUL.

A glimmering square,"
When life seems far removed,
And all its worriments
And wearying care
Have taken wings away,
How Calmness steals upon the soul,
How Peace enfolds the weary heart,
Whilst Courage comes
And takes you by the hand,
Bids you fear not,
Nor be disquieted.

O, mighty monarch Death!
Life bows at thy command;
And yet the deathless soul
Is mightier far than thou.
Behold, I fear thee not;
Come when and as thou wilt,
And I am ready.

Sweet friends, I see you, hear you not.
Life, love and all—good-bye, good-bye.

The Queen of the
Silvery Coronal

THE QUEEN OF THE SILVERY CORONAL.

FROM where in its splendor
    Yon star of the North
Shines back from the tideless Ocean,
A fond heart and true,
Through the night dark and eery,
Across the wide prairie
Is wafting me loving devotion.

THE QUEEN OF THE SILVERY CORONAL.

O, maidenly heart,
I am ill, I am lonely;
The night draweth down,
And there comes to me only
The cry of the wind,
And the sea's wild commotion.

Come breathe to me,
Breathe to me
Words sweet and low,
And wreathe for me,
Wreathe for me
Love's long ago,
And quiet this deep emotion.

Ah, sorry am I,
On my couch as I lie,
For you lonely star in the lonely sky
At watch o'er the desolate sea.
The night is so still and the sky is so wide,
And the sea a bare plain without shipping or tide,
Or even a leafless tree.

But I learn through love's art
That the star is the heart,
And it shineth alone for me.
And I dream and I dream
That each radiant gleam
A whisper of love must be.

THE QUEEN OF THE SILVERY CORONAL.

Come, heart of the North!
Come out of the star
To my home by the western sea.
It seemeth, alas! so far, so far,
'Twixt the tideless ocean and me.

Ten thousand, ten thousand
Such stars in the skies,
Could never so comfort me
As the wonderful love that glows in your eyes
So fondly and fervently.

Come follow, come follow,
Dear, little white hand!
Come follow your wonted way
O'er coif and o'er braid and o'er shining band,
As of old at the close of day.

And bring me a lily
Of purest white,
Of spotless beauty and petals rare,
To blaze like a peerless gem to-night,
In the folds of my snowy hair.

And shine, O star,
With your brightest sheen
To the waves of the tideless sea,
For I, I ween, shall the crownéd Queen
Of the Silvery Coronal be.

From where in the Orient
The light of to-day
Is already far on towards to-morrow,
Come, voice that I love,
For the shadows are thronging,
And my heart throbs with longing
One joy from the bygone to borrow.

Come over the hills
Like the dove to its homing,
Come airily soft
As the sigh of the gloaming,
And tunefully sad
As the rhythm of sorrow.

Come sing to me,
Sing to me
Songs sweet and low,

THE QUEEN OF THE SILVERY CORONAL.

And bring to me
Bring to me
Love's long ago,
For I shrink from the dread to-morrow.

Ah, sorry am I,
On my couch as I lie,
For yon lonely wind with its lonely cry
As it roams o'er the desert and lea.
The night is so cold and the desert so old,
And the mountains so wrinkled and rough and bold,
And never a sail on the sea.

But hark, and rejoice,
For the wind is the voice,
And it carolleth wild and free,
And I dream and I dream
That its notes, as they seem,
Are but whispers of love to me.

Come, voice of my love,
Come out of the wind
To my home by the western sea,
It seemeth, alas! so hard to find
The way o'er the desert to me.

Ten thousand, ten thousand
Such spirits of air
Could never bring peace to me
So tenderly, sweetly, O voice so rare,
As the sounds of your melody.

THE QUEEN OF THE SILVERY CORONAL.

Come follow, come follow,
O beautiful lips,
Come follow your wonted way
To that spot on my brow where the wild lock slips
From the braided bands astray.

And bring me a song,
That has never been sung,
From the depths where their pure souls lie
Like glittering gems on the white sands flung
By the tide as the waves roll by.

And sing, O wind,
To the forests green,   .
To the mountains, the desert and sea,
For I, I ween, shall the crownéd Queen
Of the Silvery Coronal be.

And the heart 'neath the star,
At Love's call from afar,
Came down to the western sea.
And the voice sped away
On the beams of day
Over mountain and forest and lea.

And the heart brought a lily from out of the North,
Of wondrous beauty and fabulous worth,
To wreathe in the glistening hair.
And the voice brought a song that had never been sung,
But lay like a pearl on its golden tongue
For the queenly listener there.

But the song was laid in a grave new made,
And the brow that was far more fair,
In its noisome shade must wither and fade,
And dull grow the silvery hair.

And the lily lies pressed on a cold white breast,
But the soul that was whiter than they,
Through the shadowy west has found its rest
In the realms of Elysian day.

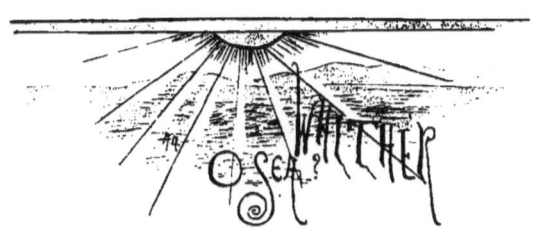

WHITHER, O SEA!

O SEA, and O, Sea!
If I sailed and I sailed
And I sailed to the west,
Would I find the far land
Where the dead are at rest?

O, Sea and O, Sea!
If I passed softly down through thy waters so blue,
If I searched all the realms of thy hidden world through,
If I trod the strange soil that no foot ever pressed,
Would I find the far land where the dead are at rest?

O, mystic Mirage!
If I watched and I watched all the long sunny day,
Anacappa's dim isle rise out of the bay   .
Like the shadowy curve of the sea's swelling breast,
Would'st thou paint me the land where the dead are at rest?

O, Mountains and Hills!
O, snow-covered height that my sad vision fills!
If I conquered thy rocks with my soul's alkahest,
If I delved and I delved through the hollow world's crest
Would I find the far land where the dead are at rest?

O, white-wingéd Snow!
O, Winds that so bitterly, bitterly blow!
If I followed and followed thy wearisome course.
If that infinite spot, thy ultimate source,
To my soul and my senses, at length, stood confessed,
Would I find the far land where the dead are at rest?

O, Sun and O, Sun!
If I rode and I rode in thy chariot of fire,
If I swept through the heavens, ever swifter and higher,
If I traversed thy course from the east to the west,
Would I find the far land where the dead are at rest?

O, sable-hued Night!
If I pierced thy dark depths to their uttermost deep,
If I sought out the spot where thy blackest shades sleep,
If midst all thy shadows I followed my quest,
Would I find the far land where the dead are at rest?

O, Mountains and Hills! O, Sun and O, Sea!
Where and O, where can the soul's aiden be?
O, mystic Mirage! O, sable-hued Night!
Whither away doth the soul wing its flight?

O, Time and O, Space!
O, Omnipotent One!
Where dwelleth the soul when its life work is done?
Is it far beyond life, beyond time, beyond thought?
I ask and I wait, but ye answer me not.

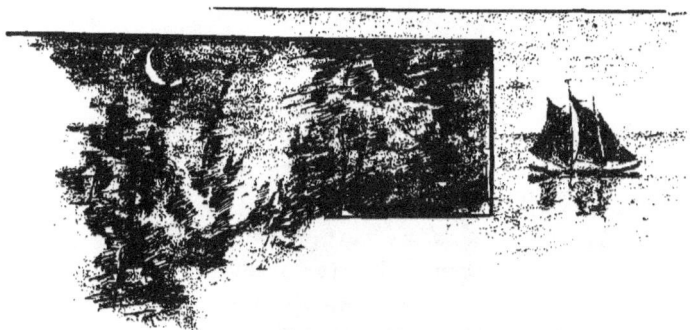

BEYOND THE SILVERY MISTS.

THERE is a land beyond the swelling seas,
　　Beyond the silvery mists,
Beyond the far horizon,
Beyond the snowy clouds,
That, rising tier on tier,
From out old Ocean's utmost verge,
Lift their weird, fantastic shapes to heaven;
Unseen by mortal eyes,
Unknown and undiscovered
It lies—Death's country.
Nor from its distant shores
Has ever message come,
Nor sight nor sound;
Unless it be that now and then,
When in some silent, dreamy hour,

BEYOND THE SILVERY MISTS.

All nature is at peace
    And the winds come creeping softly
    Out of the shadowy west,
    There fall upon the ear
    The faintly echoing tones
    Of voices we have known and loved.
    Or when within the shadow
    Of some overhanging rock,
    We sit upon the sandy beach
    And listening, listening silently,
    We find there runneth
    Through the sad sea's murmuring
    A far-off, busy hum
    As of an earnest, happy people
At their daily round of pleasure and of duty.

Or when Night drops her sombre shadows down,
And the distant stars glow fitfully,
Like phantom fires of phantom hosts
Encamped on phantom fields of battle,
And all the world seems filled
With awe and ghostliness,
There steals upon the soul
A subtle, dawning consciousness
Of life beyond the silvery mists,
Of deathless immortality.

Or yet, when on some lonely autumn day,
We sit reclining, on the fallen leaves
At some old forest monarch's foot,—

 The while the soul confused, bewildered,
 In gentlest melancholy wrapped,
 Questions its own existence and identity,—
 Borne in upon the longing heart,
 There comes a sense intangible, unreal,
 Of blest communion with Death's country.

 They say it is a silent land.
 And yet we know
 That there have passed
 Within its boundaries,
 Some of the sweetest voices
 Nature ever knew,
 And happiest souls
 That ripple forth their joy
 In merry laughter and rich melody.
 And it must surely be
 That that All-listening ear,
 Which hath attuned the music of the spheres,
 Hath also set the stars
 Which stud Death's firmament,
 To run their course in rhythmic measure;
 Hath filled Death's fields
 And groves and forests
With golden-throated songsters,
And hath wrought into the waves
That break upon that distant unknown shore

Songs full of longing,
That breathe of by-gone days,
Of loves and fond regrets,
And Life's fair memories.

They say it is a gloomy, cheerless land.
And yet the same Almighty hand
That gladdened life
With joy and sunshine,
And crowdeth
One rare beauteous day upon another,
That builded in their glorious majesty
The everlasting hills,
Touched them with grandeur and sublimity,
And wreathes them daily
In their changing lights and shadows,
That poured out Ocean's depths
And set its restless floods in motion,
That studded night
With her unnumbered brilliants,
And flecked the verdant fields
With ever blooming beauty—
That All-puissant arm,
Clothed with boundless power and resource,
Wrought Death's country also.
And since we know that every soul
Which sets its purpose high,
And presses toiling on

BEYOND THE SILVERY MISTS.

To points that rise
Still lifting to the far beyond,
Before it passes to that unknown bound,
Grows ever toward the infinite,
Becomes attuned to every subtle sense
Of grace and loveliness and beauty,
And grows the more and swifter
Where nobleness and beauty most abound,
And passes on to its new life
With quickened attributes,
Equipped for richer, rarer, higher joys,—
Since this we surely know,
There resteth then a happy certainty,
That in Death's country
It will find but freer scope
For its enlarged capacities.
The towering heights
Beyond the silvery mists
Shall overtop earth's loftiest mountains,
Death's silvery sea
Shall swell its waves
In finer curves of beauty;
Death's flowers shall fairer grow;
Death's music roll
In sweeter, nobler cadences,
And Death's eternal life
Be filled with higher, loftier aspirations,
With mightier achievements,
With joys that grow
To full and glad fruition.

And as the crowding centuries
Sweep onward in their mighty cycles,
The deathless soul,
O'er Death and Time triumphant,
Shall win to higher, grander possibilities,
Until, at length, it gain
The heights supreme, the ultimate,
Where dwells Infinity.

THE RIVER OF LIFE.

A DOWN the dark valley, adown the dark valley
    The River of Life hurries on to the sea.
No more 'neath the willows its shining waves dally,
No more linger lightly by forest and lea.

THE RIVER OF LIFE.

How changed is the sweep of its mighty on-rushing
Since the far-away hour when the glad day was new,
When it leaped into light — a tiny spring gushing,
Bedewing the soil where the wild flowers grew.

How it laughed in its beauty — a crystal clear fountain,
Far up on the heights where the morning mists hung,
And rippled so tunefully down the wild mountain
Like a silvery song on a wide silence flung.

How it sang to the fields! How it raced the swift swallows
And whirled the wild rose in its eddying play!
'Till it swept a full stream o'er its deepening shallows
And rivalled the sun as it rolled on its way.

Upborne on its bosom, my bark like a feather
Came floating, came floating adown the soft tide;
Whilst the day was delight, and the stars sang together
And decked the fair night like a beautiful bride.

The air was aglow with a luminous glory,
The lilies looked up with a gentle surprise;
On the breeze came the breath of Love's rapturous story,
And pinnacled palaces rose to the skies.

I dreamed that my bark down the soft flowing river
Would float on for aye through the ambient air;
And the future smile on through a golden forever,
And the flowers bloom eternal, unfadingly fair.

And I dreamed that the span of youth's purple-hued iris
Would never unbend from the storm-riven skies;
And that Love, though he fail, like the fabled Osiris,
Would rise with new light in his wonderful eyes.

But gone are the sunny hours, gone are the meadows,
Gone the sweet stars, and the beautiful sky;
Gone the bright day, and fallen the shadows,—
We're alone on the waters — my sad soul and I.

Adown the dark valley, adown the dark valley,
The river is hurrying on to the sea.
No more 'neath the willows its shining waves dally,
No more linger lightly by forest and lea.

How they leap and they flash! How they boil as they dash
'Gainst the cliff that frowns at their side!
How they hurl the wild moss as they threat'ningly toss
My bark to the sea's boundless tide!

And how the blast raves through its bellowing caves,
With the tempest-born demons at war!
And hark, the wild roar that swells evermore
From the Stygian isles afar!

How the sharp forkéd light crashes down through the night
'Till the heavens seem rolling on me!
How the cold cutting hail tears the quivering sail,
And stabs all the shuddering sea!

How the voices of Night in their frenzied delight
Shriek and cry o'er my shelterless head!
How the mad ocean swells as it knells and it knells
A funeral dirge o'er the dead!

And up from below, as it flits to and fro,
Like vapors that stream from the grave,
On the black breast of Night gleams a weird ghostly light
That haunts the white crest of the wave.

'Tis the fires that rise from the cavernous eyes
Of the hideous shapes of the sea,
As they slimily creep through the wastes of the deep
And breathe their hot breath upon me.

O, Soul of mine, Soul of mine! cease from thy crying!
Let the black billows yawn till their fountains lie bare!
The victory speeds where the colors are flying,
And glory finds rest where the bravest souls are.

O Soul of mine, Soul of mine! cease thy complaining!
Thou wast born of the Infinite, ages ago;
And ages on ages shall wax to their waning,
Whilst still through thy being the life currents flow.

No storms can destroy and no yawning floods drown thee!
Thou 'rt as deathless as Time and as fadeless as Truth!
For vigor and strength like an amaranth crown thee!
And Death yields the way to thy immortal youth.

O Soul of mine, Soul of mine! faint not nor falter,
Other souls have sailed over this dread sea before.
No trembling or doubt can thy destiny alter,
Then boldly press on to the blest Evermore!

There's a land where delight like a beautiful river
Shall flow on for aye through the soft dreamy air,
Where a golden bent iris shall pledge peace forever,
And the flowers bloom, eternal, unfadingly fair.

Where the happy to-day waits the blissful to-morrow,
Where Love smiles anew through his beautiful eyes;
Where joy blooms afresh through the soft dews of sorrow,
And the beckoning hope of the future ne'er dies.

THE RIVER OF LIFE.

Where the soul in a rapture of knowledge and power
May wing the wide realms of the mighty unknown,
Or crest the far heights where the awful shades lower
Which veil the vast blaze of the Infinite throne.

Hope springs from the depths like a bright Aphrodite,
And lightens the gloom that rests on our way.
There's a haven beyond and the pilot's Almighty,
And past the night's shade glows an Eternal day.